EGMONT

We bring stories to life

This edition published in Great Britain 2012 by Dean,
an imprint of Egmont UK Limited
239 Kensington High Street, London W8 6SA

Thomas the Tank Engine & Friends™

CREATED BY BRITT ALLCROFT

HiT entertainment

ISBN 978 0 6035 6669 1
51280/1
Printed in China

Thomas and the Magic Show

Based on *The Railway Series* by The Rev. W. Awdry

It was the day of the children's summer party.

Thomas was on his way to the Docks. He was to meet The Fat Controller and the Great Magician.

The Great Magician was going to do a Magic Show at the party. Thomas really wanted to be in the Show.

He pulled into the Docks.

"At the end of the party, the Great Magician is going to do a special trick," The Fat Controller told Thomas.

"I will need some very important things for it," added the Great Magician.

"You, Thomas, will collect them," boomed The Fat Controller. "And if you do your job well, you can be in the Magic Show, too!"

Thomas was very excited.

The Fat Controller told Thomas to listen very carefully. "First, you must go to Maithwaite to fetch a blue box. Then to Maron Station to collect a red carpet. And, lastly, you must pick up a yellow sheet from Knapford."

But Thomas wasn't listening. He was dreaming about being in the Magic Show!

"Can you remember all that, Thomas?" asked The Fat Controller.

"Yes, Sir!" puffed Thomas. And he chuffed away.

When Thomas arrived at Maithwaite, he met Elizabeth, who was making a delivery.

"I'm going to be in a Magic Show," tooted Thomas. "I've come to collect something for the Great Magician!"

"How jolly!" steamed Elizabeth.

On the platform was a bright red phone box.

"That must be it!" whistled Thomas.

And it was loaded on to his flatbed.

"Next stop, Maron Station!" Thomas peeped.

As Thomas puffed into Maron Station, he saw Bertie the Bus dropping off some passengers.

"Hello, Bertie!" whistled Thomas. "I'm going to be in a Magic Show!"

"That's nice," said Bertie. "What are you doing here?"

"I'm collecting something for the Great Magician!" Thomas replied, looking at a stack of yellow deckchairs on the platform. "It must be those."

So the crew loaded the deckchairs on to Thomas' flatbed, then off he chuffed again.

When Thomas arrived at Knapford Station, he told Henry all about the Magic Show.

"That's exciting!" wheeshed Henry. "Why have you come to Knapford?"

But Thomas couldn't quite remember. "I have to collect something for the Great Magician. Something blue!" he chuffed.

"There's a blue flag over there," puffed Henry.

"That must be it!" whistled Thomas. The blue flag was soon loaded on to his flatbed, and Thomas puffed off to the party.

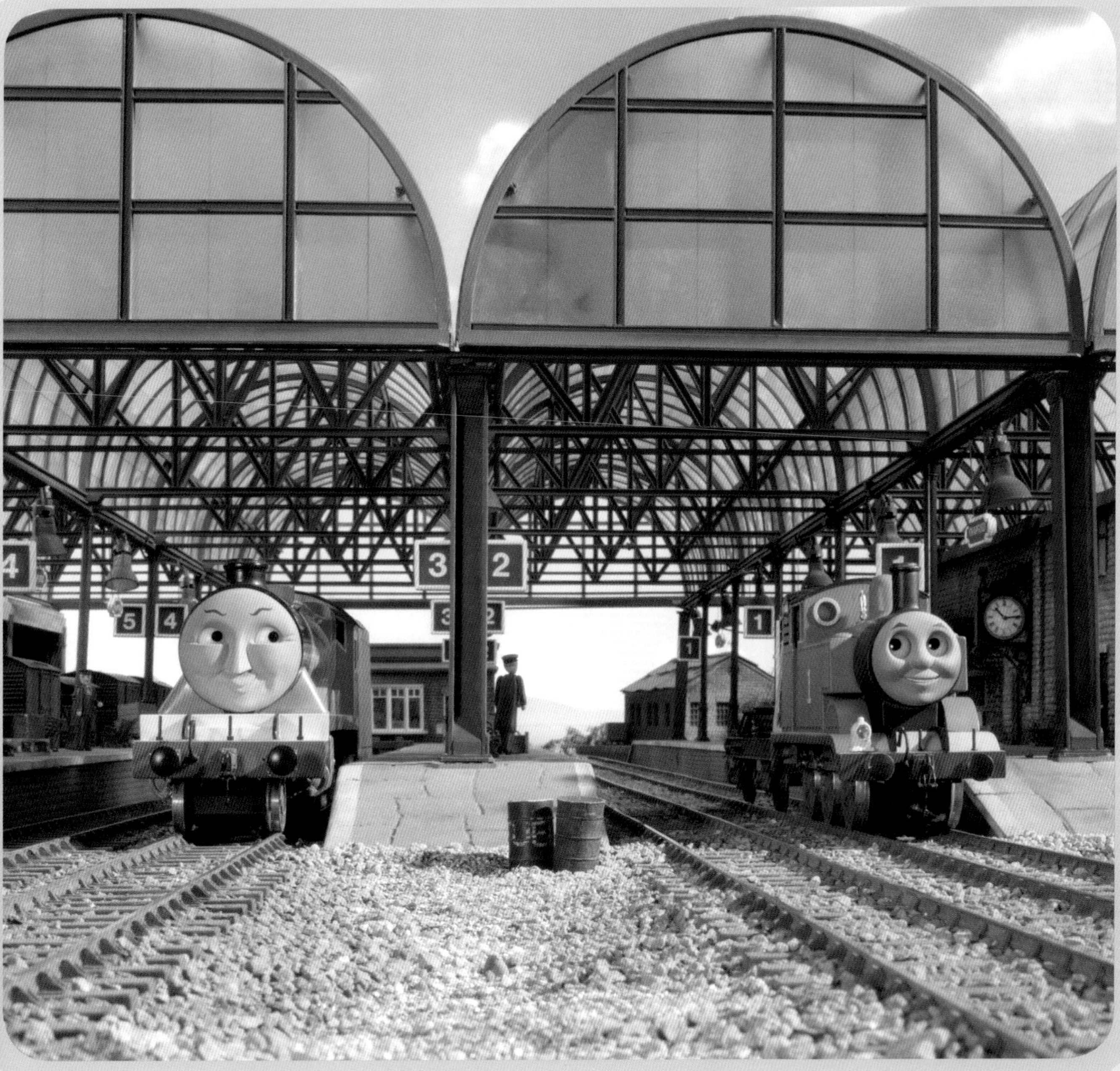
4
3 2
5 4
1

As he puffed into the station, Thomas was sure that the Great Magician was going to be very pleased with him.

The children were very excited. They couldn't wait for the Magic Show to start.

"I have brought everything you asked for," puffed Thomas, proudly. "The red phone box, the yellow deckchairs and the blue flag."

But the Great Magician was cross! "These are all the wrong things. I need my red carpet, my blue box and my big yellow sheet!" he said, angrily. "Without them, I can't do my special trick!"

Thomas felt terrible. He had been dreaming about being in the Magic Show and hadn't listened properly to The Fat Controller.

He'd puffed to all the right places . . . but picked up all the wrong things.

"I'm sorry, Great Magician," he wheeshed, sadly. "I've been a very silly engine."

It was time for the Magic Show to start. All the children were waiting.

Thomas had an idea. "Please help me unload the flatbed, then I will pick up all the right things," he asked his crew.

In no time at all, Thomas was unloaded.

He knew he would miss most of the Magic Show.

But if he hurried, Thomas could still be back in time for the special trick!

He puffed away as fast as his wheels could carry him.

First, Thomas steamed to
Maithwaite Station. "Blue box,
blue box," he whooshed to himself.

And there he saw the big blue box,
decorated with moons and stars.

Thomas was pleased.

Next, Thomas chuffed to Maron Station.
"Red carpet, red carpet," he puffed to himself.

And sure enough, rolled up on the platform was a red
carpet, ready to be loaded on to Thomas' flatbed.

"Hurry, hurry!" Thomas told his crew.

Lastly, Thomas steamed into Knapford.

"Yellow sheet, yellow sheet," he sang to himself.

And there was the big yellow sheet!

It was quickly loaded on to Thomas' flatbed, and Thomas raced back to the party!

Thomas arrived back at the summer party, just in time for the Great Magician's special trick.

He had missed almost all of the Magic Show, but Thomas was pleased that he had done his job properly.

The Great Magician began the special trick.

"And now for my best magic trick!" he announced.

The children clapped and cheered, excitedly.

Standing on the red carpet, the Great Magician put the yellow sheet in the blue box.

"Abracadabra!" he said, waving his wand.

When the Magician opened the box again, the yellow sheet had disappeared!

Then suddenly, a bunch of flowers popped out of Thomas' funnel!

The children laughed and cheered!

"Cinders and ashes!" cried Thomas. He was just as surprised as the children!

Thomas was the star of the show, after all!